Archbishop Cyril Aphrem Karim

In The Tree House

Illustrated by Brian Acquaire

Parables Books

Printed in the United States of America
April 2011 / M8439

10 9 8 7 6 5 4 3 2 1

First Edition

Edited by Tom McMillian

Book type set in Adobe Caslon Pro and Burbank

Library of Congress Cataloging-in-Publication Data is available upon request.
Library of Congress Control Number 2011922342
ISBN 978-0-9833188-0-4

 Parables & Books

Visit us online: www.parablesandbooks.com

To Christopher-Issa, Saleeba and Lydia for their inspiration.
And to Sandy Ghattas for coming up with the idea of this book.

Archbishop Cyril Aphrem Karim

These illustrations could not have been done without the vision
and inspiration provided from Archbishop Cyril, Sandy Ghattas,
and Tom McMillian.

Brian Acquaire

On a beautiful Sunday morning...

Matthew and his younger sister Sarah go to church with their parents.

Matthew quietly says his prayers with his father before they sit.

Sarah is being Sarah - she has a hard time sitting still anywhere.

As Mass is about to begin, Matthew wonders,
what's going on behind the curtain?

"There's the archbishop," says Matthew.

Matthew is excited, because he likes Mass best when
Archbishop Peter leads it.

Archbishop Peter says, "By the prayers of Your Mother and of all Your Saints..."

While gazing at the archbishop, something amazing happens - Matthew hears the calling to devote his life to God!

Suddenly, Matthew says, "That's it. That's it. Mom, I want to be an archbishop!"

As he leaves church, Matthew comes up with a brilliant idea.
"I can't wait to get started," he says to himself.

Upon arriving home, Matthew sees his best friend and neighbor, John.

Matthew shouts, "John, go ask your parents if you can play.
I'll be at the tree house in ten minutes!"

Matthew, dressed in his play clothes, bursts into Sarah's room saying "Sarah, hurry up! Stop giving mom a hard time. Let's go play!"

John hollers, "Mom and Dad said I could play!"

"John, I have a fantastic idea! Do you want to play church with us?" asks Matthew.

John loves the idea. They make their way up into the tree house.

Matthew can hardly contain himself as he instructs John and Sarah on how to set up the tree house so it looks like a church.

"Let's start by cleaning this place up. Then we can move the table up against the wall and put a juice box and plate of crackers on it, just like the altar," says Matthew.

"I'll draw a cross on the wall," continues Matthew.

"And we'll set up the pews," replies John.

"We need to make a hand cross," says Matthew.

"We can use the palm leaves to tie it together!" says John.

"Don't forget about the colorful windows!" says Sarah.

"Just a few more things. ... This is just how I remember it!" adds Matthew. "And now, if you'll help me with my robe, I'll be the archbishop!"

"Incredible! We really did it. Now this place looks just like the churc
I'll begin my sermon like Archbishop Peter did! Glory to the Father
and to the Son and to the Holy Spirit..."

Matthew, filled with excitement, repeats as much as he can remember while Sarah and John proudly cheer him on.

Over the years

Matthew grows up, playing with his friends but never forgetting the inspirational day in the tree house.

Matthew enjoys spending time with his father, especially when taking care of things around the house.

He makes his father very proud.

Matthew leads the family in prayer before dinner. "In the name of the Father and of the Son and the Holy Spirit. Lord bless our food..."

Matthew joins the church as an altar boy.

He is guided by Father Timothy.

Matthew always has time for his little sister Sarah.

When his neighbors and friends need a hand, he is the first one they go to.

Matthew continues to be active in his church and community, always motivated by his tree-house experience.

He is elevated to Reader.

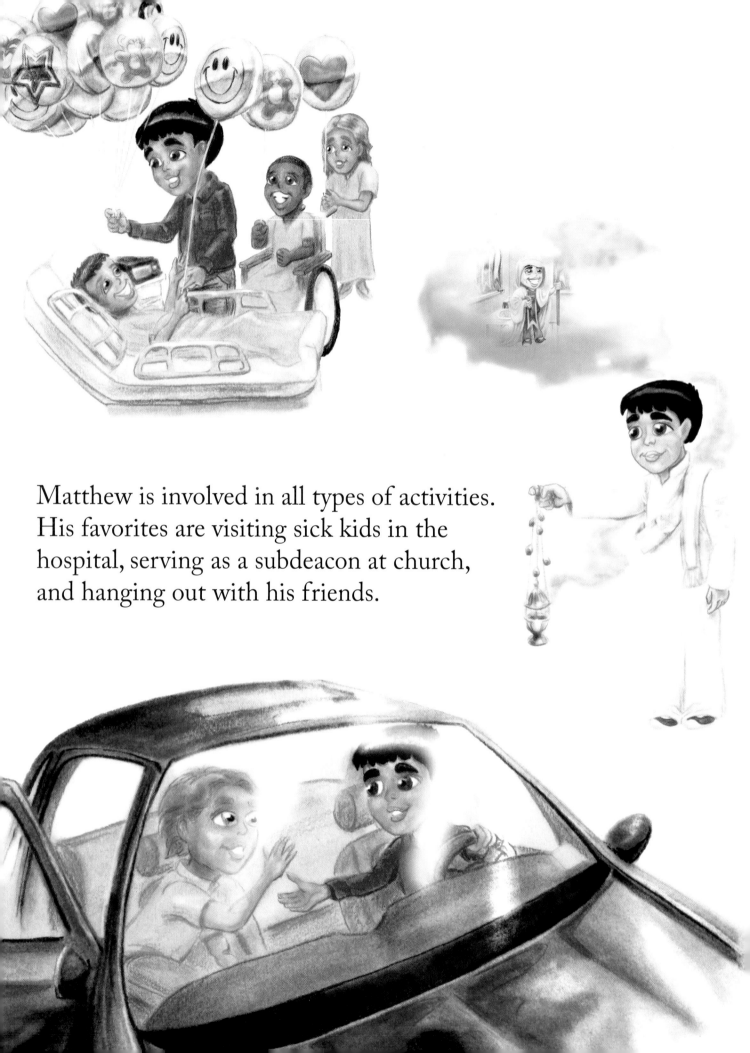

Matthew is involved in all types of activities. His favorites are visiting sick kids in the hospital, serving as a subdeacon at church, and hanging out with his friends.

Matthew attends college and spends most of his time in study and prayer groups, but also finds time to join his friends in gatherings. He graduates with high honors and is class valedictorian.

Remembering his joy in the tree house when he was just a boy, and after much prayer, Matthew joins the monastery.

In the monastery, he develops a stronger relationship with God through prayer, studies and work in the field with his brother monks.

He spends several years in the monastery before he is ordained a priest.

Upon learning that he is assigned a parish, Father Matthew prays, "God, help me do your will by serving others."

Over the years Father Matthew serves his parish and community well. He provides outstanding care for the needy and an excellent education for the children.

One day he unexpectedly receives a letter from the Patriarch.

He is to become what he played so many years ago in the tree house - an archbishop!

DEAR SPIRITUAL SON,
   YOU HAVE BEEN SELECTED TO
BECOME A BISHOP.

MAY THE LORD BLESS YOU,
PATRIARCH OF ANTIOCH
AND ALL THE EAST

"By the prayers of Your Mother and of all Your Saints..."

Author's Note

Priesthood is a calling from God which comes in different ways and through different people. From my personal experience, I can say that no power can stand against God's calling. When I joined the seminary at a young age my family was against my decision, but God's grace helped me overcome all difficulties.

By dressing as a priest or imitating a bishop, an innocent child may in reality be taking his first step in a journey toward becoming a priest committed to do God's work on earth.

My hope is that Matthew's story will inspire a few children to contemplate the priesthood and offer themselves as workers in His Vineyard.

Cyril Aphrem Karim